I Love Seeds

Written by
Julie Smithwick

Words brought to Life by
Marie Fritz Perry

Published by
Hasmark Publishing, judy@hasmarkservices.com

Illustrations
Marie Fritz Perry

Book Layout
Anne Karklins
annekarklins@gmail.com

ISBN: 978-1-988071-83-1
ISBN: 1988071836

Dream Big!
Julie

This book is dedicated to all good seeds.

With a full heart, thank you to all of my "teachers" over the years who have planted wonderful seeds in me. And a special thank you to my teachers who are still teaching me…how seeds grow. ☺

Hi there! My name is Bear.
I love seeds! I love planting
and doing good deeds.
I simply love…seeds.

Where I want to plant seeds,
there are almost always weeds.
Thank goodness I know,
how seeds and weeds grow.

I know what seeds are worth,
so I always spend time preparing the earth.
I find and pull weeds.
I enjoy making room for my wonderful seeds.

Weeds are no more!

It's time to plant seeds galore!

The earth is prepared, it's a beautiful sight.

What do I need now?

Water, time, and light.

I water the seeds.
God shines The Light.

I…wait.

I always give my seeds the time they need.

I don't beg seeds, or plead.

I know my seeds grow at just the right speed.

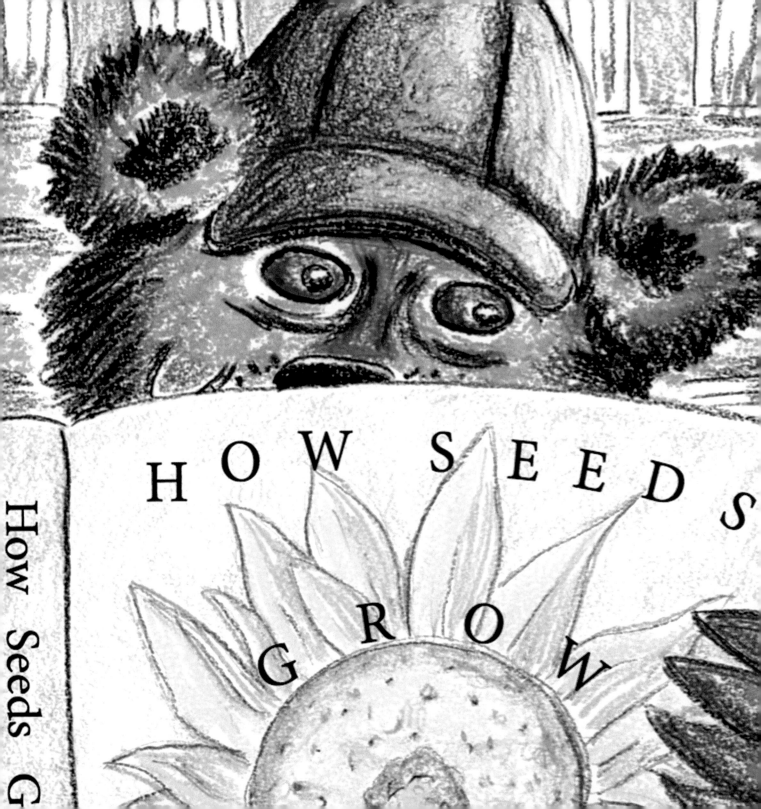

HOW SEEDS

GROW

Sheep looks at Goose, "Whatcha doin' Bear?"
"I'm watchin' my seeds I planted right there."
"I don't see seeds," Goose whispered to Sheep.

No one can see what lies beneath.

"Just wait," I said loud and clear.
"Seeds are most certainly planted right there."

"Seeds, sneads and fiddle-fleads!
You always say you're planting seeds.
Why don't we ever see your seeds grow?
C'mon Sheep, let's go!"

"You don't see because you don't wait."
But Goose and Sheep were already out the gate.
"I will wait," I said to myself.
"For surely I know, my seeds always grow."

You see, I know things:

(1) I know I took my seeds off the shelf.

(2) I know I planted them all by myself.

(3) I know I planted beautiful flowers.

(4) I know they are growing this very hour.

(5) I know others cannot see my seeds.

(6) I know it's my job to water and keep out the weeds.

So...I tend my garden.

I waved good-bye and hummed a tune.

I worked in my garden all afternoon.

Going home, I refused to doubt.

And the very next day,

What did I find? Sprouts!

Oh the fun of seeing them start!
This time truly warms my heart.
They need special care
at the time of their birth,
right when they start to peek
through the earth.
I always keep the water comin'.
I know my seeds are rapidly growin'.

And when it's time,
what do I always find?
Beautiful flowers
of every kind!

The same ones I dreamed in my mind.

Thankful to see,
but more thankful to know,
a long, long time ago…
someone special
taught me how seeds grow.

Made in the USA
San Bernardino, CA
16 February 2018